THEY MAY LAUGH

Dr. Lena Johnson

PAGE PUBLISHING
Conneaut Lake, PA

First originally published by Page Publishing 2022

ISBN 978-1-6624-8846-7 (pbk)
ISBN 978-1-6624-8845-0 (digital)

Printed in the United States of America

Dedicated to my daughter Libby, my talented, smart, and unique inspiration for this book.

Standing alone in the schoolyard before the bell rings, I can hear other students giggle as a girl asks me,

1

"Why are you dressed like that?"

5

My answer is simple…

"You may laugh,
You may tease.
But I am who I am,
And that is who I want to be."

While waiting in line for lunch in the cafeteria, two boys, laughing, ask me,

"Are you a boy or a girl?"

My answer is simple…

My answer is simple.

"You may laugh,
You may tease.
But I am who I am,
And that is who I want
to be."

Sitting in the grass with my headphones on, I sing to myself as the other kids play four square, climb the jungle gym, laugh, and joke.

"Where are your friends?" they ask.

"Why do you sing to yourself?"

14

My answer is simple…

"You may laugh,
You may tease.
But I am who I am,
And that is who I want to be."

My answer is still simple.

After school, I am alone again, waiting for the bus to take me home. I draw in my journal, my headphones on, pretending I am somewhere else.

My answer is still simple…

They may laugh.

"They may laugh,
They may tease.
But I am still who I am,
And that is who I want to be.
I am the *one* and *only*.
I am me!"

Afterword

No one wants to think that their child may feel alone, different, depressed, or suicidal. The reality is that growing up is hard, and learning to be who you want to be and who you are is even harder. Reassurance, understanding, and positivity are key in encouraging our kids to be accepting of themselves, others, and all of life's differences. Cherish the moments you have with your children, with their friends, and with others you meet along the way. Seek help if you or someone you know is feeling alone, depressed, or suicidal. There is always someone out there who cares about you!

About the Author

Lena Johnson was born and raised in Bremerton in the beautiful evergreen state of Washington. Lena has three amazing kids and an amazing husband, each contributing to her book ideas. Lena's inspiration for this book comes from her youngest child, who is truly a unique soul, happy, and carefree. Spending time with her family and friends is always cherished. When Lena isn't spending time with her friends and family, you can almost always find her sitting on her deck, drinking coffee with her pudgy black pug, Sumo.